# The Explorers of Lost Lane

## The Magic Room

Amy Joy & CN James

Tenterhook Books, LLC · Akron, Ohio

 Published by Tenterhook Books, LLC. Akron, Ohio.

For permission and bulk order inquiries, please contact the authors at info@tenterhookbooks.com.



ISBN-13: 9781696936828

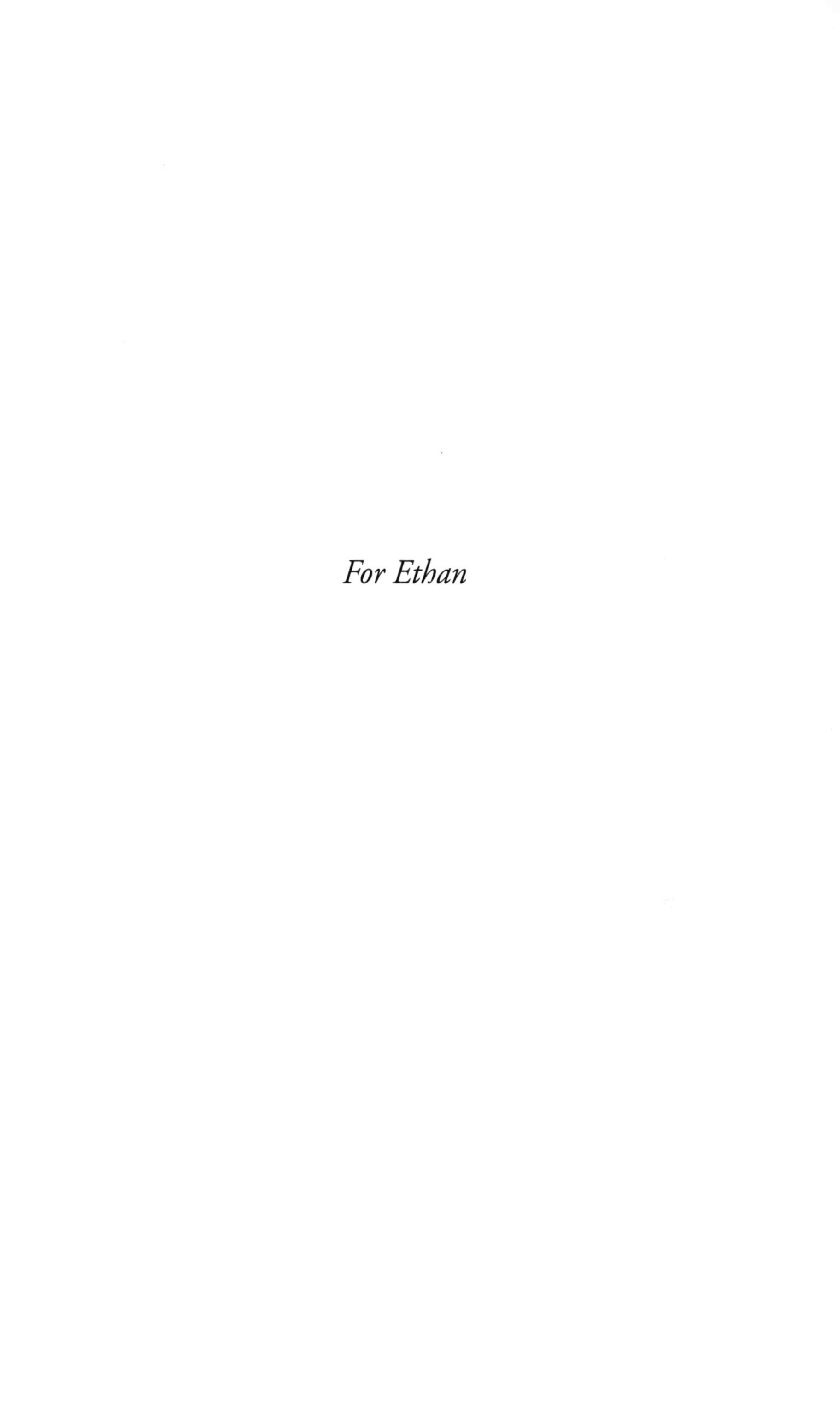

*For Ethan*

## Welcome Explorers!

When you finish the story, be sure to check out the discussion questions and activities in the back of the book.

Also, ask an adult to go online to tenterhookbooks.com/explorers and download coloring pages, activity sheets, and more!

# Prologue

No one ever moved to Lost Lane—not on purpose anyway. The houses were cheap, but all lay empty. All except one. In this home lived a family of four: a mom and dad and their two kids, Spencer, and his little sister, Emma, who was born in the house just after they moved in. The house was very old, but charming, and it was far more than the family could have afforded anywhere else. And like all those that lived on the lane before them, they experienced strange, unexplainable things. But unlike the rest, the parents chose to ignore it. And the children learned to simply live with it. It was just the quirks of an old house, Spencer told himself, trying to explain it away the way his parents always did. And this worked just fine. That is, until a new family moved in across the street.

# 1

## Spencer

Spencer Daniels was a logical sort of guy. He had long since given up believing in all the silly make-believe stuff his little sister did. Unlike Emma, he knew there was no such thing as fairies and unicorns. And he knew that magic was a trick of the eye. But with his acceptance of these things came a sadness he just couldn't shake.

Spencer was an average student, but quiet at school. He would watch as other kids would compare the new things their parents would buy them even when it wasn't their birthdays or Christmas. And after winter, spring, and summer breaks, he'd hear them talk excitedly about all the places they had been and wonderful things they had done. Spencer didn't know how to talk to these kids.

Once a year, Spencer was happy when his parents were able to scrape together enough money to take a few days off to take him and his little sister, Emma, to the zoo and water park. They'd live like kings on those days, eating out and spending the entire time together.

But Spencer knew that these were things that other kids could do easily and often, and they didn't find it as special as he did. He rarely wore new clothes, and he didn't have the latest designer anything. And that was okay by him. Except he didn't have any friends.

Most of the time, the other kids didn't pay him any attention. That is, except on days that he'd build something special. Spencer wasn't sure that he liked the attention, but he couldn't help it. He loved to make things.

While the teacher would be lecturing, his mind would wander off, creating. And sometimes, while the other students were taking notes, Spencer would be drawing up plans. His dad worked in construction, and Spencer liked to build with the scraps of wood and old tools his dad gave him. But his interest wasn't limited to wood. Spencer liked to create with just about anything he could get his hands on—scraps of paper, a bit of glue, tape, string—you name it, he could make something out of it.

And when the teacher would assign them a project—like creating a simple box to collect their Valentines, Spencer couldn't help it: his mind just got carried away. And then next thing you knew, out of an old shoe box and some construction paper, he'd created an entire Valentine machine ready to swallow down his classmates' Valentines and neatly organize them according to size and weight.

This everyone noticed. And Spencer would alternately beam and blush at the attention. But in a short while the projects would be put away, and Spencer would fade out of notice once more.

It was springtime, just days before the school year's end. The yellow school bus dropped him and his sister off at the end of the street, and Spencer pulled the key out from the rope around his neck as he and Emma trudged down the lane to their house.

But as they did, something new caught his eye. In the yard of the house across the street, the "For Sale" sign that had stood for as long as he could remember was gone. And a moving van was parked in its gravel drive.

# 2

# Ollie

Ollie Johnson never really had any close friends, unless you counted his younger sister, Izzy. He and Izzy got along alright, despite the fact that they were interested in very different things. But she tolerated his long-winded speeches about the things he loved, and he listened to hers, though often neither of them really had a clue what the other was talking about.

Ollie's parents couldn't afford much, but it wasn't this that separated him from his classmates. He simply had nothing to talk to them about. You see, Ollie didn't care about football, basketball, or soccer the way other kids did. All he cared about was music and dancing. And for him, the two were one in the same because Ollie loved to make music with his feet.

His parents didn't have the time or money to drop Ollie off at dance lessons. And Ollie wasn't sure that he'd feel comfortable at lessons anyway, because for some reason, he heard that they were filled with girls. But these setbacks didn't stop Ollie from dancing.

For Christmas one year, Ollie's parents had given him a collection of old Fred Astaire movies—from the days when films were all black and white—and Ollie watched those movies over and over and over again, mimicking the dancers' every move. And though few ever got to witness it, Ollie was in fact a very fine dancer. He had a sense of rhythm quite uncommon for a boy his age.

This was why he was so excited about the new house they were moving into. It had wooden floors and a cement basement! His grandmother's house, where he had lived with his parents for as long as he could remember, was carpeted. That is, except for tiny bits of linoleum in the kitchen and bathroom. And grandma didn't like him scuffing up her linoleum.

This didn't provide Ollie much opportunity to practice away from the watchful eyes of the neighborhood kids. Sometimes, after everyone had gone in for supper, he'd head out to the street and dance until dinnertime had ended. But these moments were rare, and never long enough.

But wood! He couldn't wait to get his feet on those floors! And if Mom and Dad complained, he knew he could always go into the basement and let his beat-up old dress shoes tap away on the hard concrete. And if that didn't work, he could go outside. Because Mom and Dad said this old street was deserted. Finally, he could dance to his heart's content without any onlookers or critics. Ollie couldn't wait!

And that's why, as he carried his few treasured belongings from the car to the new house, he paused when he saw the two kids walking down the street towards him. There was only one place they could be going, and that was to the house right across the street.

# 3

## Izzy

Ollie's younger sister, Izzy, didn't see the other two children as they made their way down the street into the house opposite her. She was lost, as always, in her mind, this time dreaming about all she could do with the wonderful new space they were moving into. Back at grandma's, she and Ollie had to share a room—and a small one at that. There was little space for them to make their own, and even less room for her to set up her equipment and conduct her experiments. *Finally, I can be a real scientist,* she thought. *And maybe someday, I'll even get a real microscope!*

All Izzy had wanted for her last birthday was

a microscope. And when she opened the box that day and saw that somehow her parents had managed to get her one, Izzy was overjoyed. That is, until she tried it.

In their defense, it did magnify things, so it was, in fact, a microscope. But all it could do was take things she could already see and bring them into sharper focus. And this didn't make Izzy as happy as her parents had hoped, though she tried hard to fake enthusiasm. For Izzy had really hoped that at last she would be able to see things that were so small, they couldn't be viewed by the naked eye. Things like cells, and germs, and bugs too small to see. What she didn't know was that those types of microscopes were very expensive, and she probably wouldn't have the opportunity to use one for many, many years, when she went off to college.

Though disappointed, Izzy was smart, and she found other ways to see and learn about the things she wanted. She had a library card, and she knew how to use it. The town library was a short walk from their elementary school, and often she and Ollie would walk there after school and read for the hour or so before their Mom or Dad would stop by to pick them up on their way home from work.

But now that they were moving into the new house, they'd have a new library with new books and new things to learn. And the best part was that not only would they be able to walk to this new library from school, but they could walk home afterwards as well, as it was only a few blocks away. This meant, of course, that even in the summer, Izzy could go there as often as she wanted.

Though their parents had described the home in great detail, today was the first day Izzy and Ollie actually got to see it for themselves. Ollie had already claimed the larger of the two kids' rooms, but Izzy didn't mind. Whoever had lived in her room last had already painted it purple, and that was just fine with Izzy, who loved the color as well.

Walking into her new room for the first time, Izzy piled her things along one wall, leaving room for the bed that would be moved in later. Then she began to explore.

There wasn't much to see. The room was narrow and rectangular, with a built-in dresser and cabinet to hang things above it near the door. On the far wall, there was a built-in bookshelf below the window. "Yes!" she said happily. "I'll fill you later," she added, turning to face the wall to its left.

It was this wall, the empty one of the left side of the room, which especially excited her. For at the bottom of this wall was a curious panel, no more than two feet tall, with a tiny picture of an elephant drawn on it in pink crayon. "Now *that* will require further investigation," she said out loud to herself.

And with that, she turned and began rooting through her boxes in search of her flashlight.

# 4

## Emma

The little girl didn't see her as she carried her things into the house, but that didn't dampen Emma's excitement. Emma had lived her entire life in the house on Lost Lane, and in all that time the house across the street had been deserted. But now, at last, a family was moving in. And the little girl was her age. Emma was certain of it!

She bounded into the house singing, "I'm gonna have a friend! I'm gonna have a friend!" Tossing her backpack onto the kitchen table, she turned back to look up at her brother. "Do you think we can go over there now, Spencer?"

"Not now. They're still moving in." Spencer opened the refrigerator door and looked around inside it until he found a jar of pickles.

"Did you see them? They're our age, Spence!"

"You don't know that. That girl looked at least a year older than you." He pulled a pickle from the jar and took a bite, then tightened the lid and put the jar back in its place.

"So?" she said, looking hurt. "That doesn't mean she won't want to play."

"Don't get your hopes up," he said, slamming the refrigerator door shut.

"You're always so serious! You don't even know how to play anymore."

Spencer's voice came muffled as he tried to talk through a half-chewed pickle. "Do too."

"Na uh!"

"I do too know how to play." He paused to swallow down his most recent bite, then said: "But I have to be serious too. Mom and Dad can't afford a babysitter. It's up to me. I have to be responsible."

"Can't I just go over and say 'hi?'"

"No."

"Just an itsy-bitsy two second *hi*?" She flashed him her cutest, most innocent looking smile.

"No."

"Pleeeeeeeese?"

"No."

"Fine," she huffed. "I'm going to my room." And grabbing her backpack once more, off she went.

* * *

Inside her room, Emma couldn't help but peek out the window at the house across the street. "She's not that much older than me," she said to herself.

She watched the little girl pull boxes and bags from the moving van and carry them into the house across the street. She hoped that the girl might happen to look up and see her in the second story window and wave. And then she could run outside and the two would immediately become best friends (she was pretty sure that was how it worked). But the girl didn't look up.

Emma knocked on her window, hoping to

catch the girl's attention. To Emma's surprise, there came a return knock. But it came not from across the street, but from behind her.

She spun around expecting to see her brother. But there was no one there.

Deciding it must have been Spencer joking around, Emma turned back to the window and watched as the girl pulled a stack of cardboard boxes from the truck. She wanted so badly to learn the new girl's name and to find out what she was like. But the girl walked back to the house and the door shut behind her.

Engines started below, and the moving van and an old brown car that had been parked out in the street began to move. And before Emma could even pry her eyes from the door where the girl had disappeared, the vehicles had taken off down the street.

It came from the wall beside her!

## *THUD!*

Emma wanted to scream, but the scream caught in her throat as thumping footsteps came, one after another. Like someone—or something—was walking inside her bedroom wall!

They were moving away from her, towards the door, but they seemed to stop abruptly by the closet.

SMASH!

The door of her closet shook as something bashed against it. Whatever it was, it was inside her closet!

# 5

# The Monster in the Closet

Emma found her voice at last. "SPENCER!" she shrieked.

Spencer burst into the room. The pastel-colored butterflies that hung from her ceiling swayed overhead. "What?" he said, his eyes anxiously scanning the room.

Nearly everything in Emma's room—the walls, rug, bedding, clothes, toys—were pink, and it took a moment for his eyes to find her, curled up on the bed with a pink blanket wrapped around her.

Emma pulled her knees up tighter under her chin. "Something's in my closet!" she said, pointing at the closet door.

Spencer looked at her skeptically. "This isn't one of your—"

"Shhh!" She lowered her voice to a whisper. *"Listen!"*

Anxious moments passed.

Nothing.

N o t h i n g.

N o t h i n g.

"What am I listening for?" Spencer said loudly.

"Spencer, *shh!* It will know we're here!"

"What?"

"The thing inside my closet!" Her eyes were wide. "I think it was trying to get out."

"Maybe it's the pony you claim lives in there? He's decided the closet is too small for him."

"That's not funny, Spencer!"

The anxiety Spencer felt upon entering the room had left him. Emma was always talking about imaginary friends, and she told stories of things she said had happened, when, of course, they had not. She lunched with fairies often and held tea parties with unicorns. This was nothing new.

"I really don't have time for this," he said, opening the closet.

Emma gasped and threw the blanket over her head.

"There's nothing here," he said, stepping aside to prove it.

Emma peeked through the blanket fibers. "What if it's a ghost?" she asked.

"It's not a ghost."

"How do you know?"

"Ghosts don't live in closets."

Emma threw the blanket off. "I'm not a baby, Spencer."

"Think about it: if it were a ghost, it could walk through the door. It wouldn't be stuck in the closet."

"Maybe they don't all work that way?"

Spencer huffed."If you don't mind, I have some *real* things I'd like to work on."

And with that, he turned and left the room.

* * *

The closet door was still ajar. Emma stared at it from her place on the bed. She knew what she heard. Yes, she liked to imagine all kinds of things. It made life more fun. But this was not her imagination. Something real had been inside her closet moments ago, and she was certain it had wanted to get out.

She sat there for what felt like a really long time, staring at the gap between the door frame and the open door, trying to peer inside. She watched it, waiting for something inside to rustle or reach a hand out, but the closet was now quiet.

Slowly, she inched down the bed towards it. Then she slid off the mattress, onto the floor, and crawled over to it. She peeked inside.

Nothing.

Just her clothes, some shoes, and—

"I don't remember those," she said aloud as she reached in and pulled out a pair of fluffy, white bunny slippers with long floppy ears. She smiled as she looked them over. Then, deciding she must have either forgotten she had them or that they were a surprise gift from her mom, she stood up and slipped them on. They fit perfectly.

They were soft and squishy, and she danced about in them gleefully.

*Shhhhhfffft*

*BUMP!*

It came from inside the closet!

Emma quickly swirled around to face the door.

She stared at it for what felt like a long time. Then she drew a deep breath and stepped towards it.

As she reached the door, a small, gray, tentacle-like appendage reached out and tickled her on the nose.

Emma let out a happy giggle. Then she gently took and greeted the hand-like trunk. "Oh, hello there, little elephant!" she said.

# 6

# Closet Monsters Love PB&J

Back in his room, Spencer tried to focus on his latest project, but his mind was distracted. First, thinking about Emma and her foolish make-believe. Second, thinking about the final days of school and the upcoming track-and-field day. At his school, most of the last day of school events were silly relays like pass-the-egg on a spoon and the three-legged race. The teachers seemed to think they were great fun, and most of the kids did too, but for Spencer the upcoming day of events made him anxious. It meant watching a lot of other kids quickly choose their best friends for partners, and him, silently being left behind. *Who wants to tie their leg to someone else anyway?* he thought, sourly. *It's just a stupid baby game.*

He pushed the tools aside on his desk and scooted his chair back. His parents wouldn't be home for hours still, and his stomach was grumbling, despite the pickle. A snack would help him think better, he resolved.

Head down, he wandered into the kitchen. There he found his sister, rummaging through the cupboards. On her feet were a strange, floppy-eared pair of bunny slippers.

"What's with the slippers?"

"I found them in my closet."

Spencer huffed. It always seemed Emma was getting special treats from his parents just because she was the youngest. He watched as she slopped jelly onto a piece of bread. "I thought you had a snack when we got home?"

"I did. This is for my elephant."

"Of course," he said, rolling his eyes. Emma had moved on to globbing peanut butter onto a second piece of bread. "What makes you think elephants like peanut butter and jelly sandwiches?"

"I don't *think* they do; I *know* they do."

"Oh really. How's that?"

"Because she ate my leftover one, from lunch. She found it in my backpack and nom-nom-nom, gobbled it up."

Spencer sighed. "You know, if you want people to believe your stories, you have to make up stuff that's even *remotely* possible. An elephant would never fit in our *living room*, let alone your bedroom."

"I know *that.* But it's not a *normal* elephant. It's a *tiny* one."

"Of course. What was I thinking?" he said, growing more annoyed by the moment.

The knife clinked inside the empty peanut butter jar. "Oh no!" Emma cried. "It's gone. Now what do I do?"

"Guess you'll have to make her an *imaginary* sandwich."

"It's not funny, Spencer! She won't get full on imaginary sandwiches."

Spencer pulled an apple from the fridge and grabbed a napkin from the table. "Clean up that mess when you're done," he said, eying the crumbs and gooey peanut butter and jelly that now decorated the counter. "I'm not getting yelled at again because you made a mess."

He sighed and shook his head as he headed back to his room. He didn't know why, but it bothered him that Emma was always so lost in her own imagination. It seemed like she was setting herself up for future disappointment. Someday she'd have to learn about the real world.

But for now, somehow, it just made him feel lonelier.

# 7

## Emma's Tiny Elephant

Emma swished her arm over the counter, knocking the crumbs to the floor. Then she grabbed up the sandwich and hurried back to her room. She knew that one sandwich wouldn't be enough to keep her new elephant friend happy—after all, it was the size of large dog—but she hoped it would keep her around at least a little while longer. Her footsteps quickened as she considered the fact that for all she knew, the elephant had already left.

But when she opened the door, there she was, smiling as ever and surrounded by a mess of Emma's things. "My, you have been busy,"

Emma said, laughing as she pulled a pink t-shirt from the elephant's back. "If you want some clothes, we may have to get you some of your own," she told the elephant. "Mine are all too small for you."

The elephant's eyes had lit upon the peanut butter and jelly sandwich the moment Emma opened the door. She reached out her trunk for it, curling the end around it, and shoved it into her mouth. Then she cooed for more.

"I'm sorry. I don't have any more."

The elephant's smile became a pout.

"Maybe Mom or Dad can pick up more? I can probably get you more tomorrow."

This did not appear to cheer her. Her little gray mouth curled and her brow furrowed. She seemed to be deep in thought. Then she smiled suddenly, reached out her trunk, lifted Emma onto her back, and ran full on into Emma's open closet.

# 8

# The Johnson House Ghost

With his belongings now piled high along one wall, Ollie Johnson had no sooner begun to tap around on the wooden floor in his new bedroom when he heard an unexpected sound: a giggle, like that of a small child. He stopped and listened carefully. But all was quiet. At first, he thought he must have imagined it. But just as he began to tap again, a new sound came: a thumping like something loud running around inside his bedroom walls.

Ollie dashed from the room. He was many things, but brave was really not one of them. Knocking briskly on his sister's door, his eyes darted repeatedly back to his own bedroom, where he half-expected to see a monster running after him.

"Come in," Izzy called.

Ollie whipped open the door, tucked himself inside, and quickly closed it behind him. Then he stood there with his back up against it. "So, um, when did Mom and Dad say they'd be home?"

"Not till much later. They have to return the van and go back to Grandma's to make sure we didn't forget anything important."

Ollie swallowed nervously. "Hey, uh, you haven't heard anything weird lately, uh, have you?"

Izzy was knelt on the floor, poking about a panel at the bottom end of the left wall. A flashlight lay on the floor next to her. "Like what?" she asked without looking up.

"Uh, I don't know. Anything? Ghosts maybe?"

This caused her to turn. "Really? What makes you think there's ghosts?"

"Giggling. Do ghosts giggle?"

She shrugged. "Sometimes."

"And thumping. It sounded big. Running. Probably coming to eat me."

"Ghosts don't eat people," Izzy said, a serious look on her face. "But if there are ghosts, that would be pretty amazing."

Ollie's eyes widened. "You scare me sometimes."

Izzy smiled. "I'll check that out next. First, I gotta figure this out," she said, turning back to the wall.

"What's with the elephant?" Ollie asked, eying the hand-drawn image at the top left of the panel.

Izzy ran her fingers over it. "It's crayon, so I guess this must have been a kid's room."

"Huh. Well, while you investigate in here, I'm gonna head outside and see how the road is for dancing." He pressed his ear against the door briefly, listening for monsters. "Let me know if you find anything."

"Will do," she said, tapping the panel curiously. She was so preoccupied that she didn't even notice as her brother flung the door open and closed it quickly behind him.

"Ah ha!" she said, as she finally got the panel to move. "Ollie, check this out!" She pushed the panel aside and excitedly crawled inside. "Ollie?" she called behind her.

But Ollie was already gone.

# 9

## Hide and Seek

Spencer could hear Emma talking and laughing to her imaginary friend in the room next to his. Then there was a loud thumping like she was jumping around the room. Spencer pushed his projects aside once more. He couldn't concentrate with all these distractions. He banged on the wall and hollered for her to cut it out. When he got no response, he walked out of the room banged on her bedroom door.

All had now gone quiet, but Spencer wasn't ready to let it go. He needed to tell her to stop bothering him. He banged and called again, "I'm gonna tell Mom you wouldn't listen to me!"

This time, when she didn't answer, he opened the door. Clothes and toys were everywhere. Over the bed, across the room, on top of the lamp. "If Mom sees this, you are gonna be in so much trouble!" He turned to the closet, assuming she must be hiding there. "You'd better get out here and start cleaning this up," he hollered, picking up shirts and dresses piled in heaps inside the closet. "Emma? Where are you?"

He turned away from the closet, walked the two steps across the room, got down onto the floor, and looked underneath the bed. When he didn't find her there, he grew more impatient. Everything was a game with her.

"I'm not playing, Emma! Get out here!" he called as he left the room. He imagined her giggling as she listened to him, forced once again into playing her silly games.

He searched all her standard hiding spots: the hamper in the bathroom, the linen closet, behind the living room couch, under the kitchen table, the coat closet by the front door.

He should have found her by now. Her

imagination might be amazing when it came to creating stories and invisible friends, but not so when it came to finding creative hiding spots. She was always easy to find.

Anger began to boil within him. She knew she wasn't allowed outside without letting him know first. He glanced out the front window. Then he checked the back. When he didn't see her, he opened the back door and headed out into the backyard. "Emma, this isn't funny! You aren't allowed outside without telling me. Where are you?"

Panic suddenly replaced his anger. She wasn't there. The house and yard were small and he had searched through the only places she could have been hiding. She was gone.

Frantically, he circled the house again, checking all the spots she had been known to hide in the past and all the best places she had seen him hide in when they played hide-and-seek. All were empty.

On his third trip around the house, he eyed the new neighbor boy in the street. He appeared to have been dancing, but stopped now to look at him. “You lose something?” the boy shouted.

“Yeah, my little sister.”

# 10

## The Search for Emma

There were no cars parked outside the boy's house, and Ollie knew immediately that this meant Spencer was likely in the same position he was: as the older brother, if anything happened to his sister, he was responsible. "I can help you look," he called to the boy across the street.

"Really?"

Ollie thought the boy looked surprised, though he couldn't imagine why. "Sure, why not?"

"Thanks. I'm Spencer," he said, walking to meet him in the street.

"Ollie. Ollie Johnson."

"I've searched everywhere. I really don't know where she could have gone." But just then his eyes settled on the house across the street. "Oh no. Unless . . ."

"What?"

"She really wanted to meet your sister."

"Oh, well, I didn't see her come by here, but I guess it doesn't hurt to check."

The two started up the Johnson's drive, and as they drew closer to the house, Ollie grew increasingly nervous. He hadn't yet forgotten what had driven him outside. "So," he said awkwardly, "you haven't heard any stories about this house, uh, you know, being haunted, have you?"

"Oh, don't tell me you believe the stories?"

"There are stories? I knew it!" he said, throwing his hands into the air.

"They say that about both our houses. But I've lived here for years. Trust me; it's just the sounds of an old house."

Ollie wasn't convinced. "Do old houses giggle?"

Spencer raised an eyebrow at him, wondering now what sort of person he was talking to. Did he have a wild imagination like Emma?

"Well this one giggled. I swear." With that, Ollie opened the front door and put out a hand to invite him inside. "You first."

Spencer wasn't sure what to think, for the boy seemed genuinely nervous about entering the house. But he stepped inside, and Ollie followed close behind.

"Izzy!" Ollie called from the entryway. But Izzy didn't answer. In fact, the house was completely silent.

And then suddenly, there was a rustling coming from the kitchen.

Ollie stood frozen, his eyes wide.

"It's probably just your sister," Spencer said. "Come on."

Ollie trailed behind. "You don't understand. Izzy's working on trying to figure out how to open a weird panel in her new bedroom. She wouldn't come out even for food until she had it figured out."

Spencer wasn't sure what Ollie was talking

about. But before he could ask, a voice came from the kitchen. It sang, "Pink fluffy clouds, pretty unicorn."

Spencer's heart sank. He stopped and looked to Ollie, who initially stayed fixed in place, a confused expression on his face. But Spencer frowned and shook his head. Then he followed the sound of the voice, and Ollie once again came along.

And sure enough, Ollie was right. For inside the kitchen was not, in fact, Izzy. Instead, there was a freshly slopped together peanut butter and jelly sandwich next to several of the Johnson's butter knives and spoons. The counter was a mess. And the mess-maker was currently working on making a second peanut butter and jelly sandwich to add to the plate.

# 11

# Little sisters can be monsters

"Oh, hi Spencer!" Emma said gleefully when she saw her brother. For some reason, he didn't look happy.

"Emma, what are you doing here?"

"Playing hide-and-seek with my elephant," she said innocently.

"Is that what she calls making peanut butter and jelly sandwiches?" Ollie asked. "Cuz I don't think my mom and dad will be too happy if she brought an elephant into our new house."

Spencer looked at him skeptically, then shook his head. "It's not true. She doesn't have a pet elephant."

"Na huh, Spence. She's in the other room."

"Where's Izzy?" Ollie interjected.

"Who's Izzy?" Emma said.

Ollie looked surprised. "Izzy's my sister. You haven't seen her?"

Emma shook her head.

"What are you doing, Emma?"

"Relax Spence. I'm just making sandwiches for my elephant."

"I can see that. Why are you doing it in someone else's house?"

"I—" her voice broke off as her eyes darted from Spencer to Ollie, and then around the room to the many boxes that were still stacked every which way. She hadn't even noticed them until now. "I—I didn't know. My elephant brought me here. I thought it was her house. She has a pretty purple room—I—I thought. I thought it was hers," she repeated. She had stopped spreading peanut butter onto the bread and looked instead as though she might cry.

"It's okay," Ollie said. "No harm done. Hi," he said, waving. "I'm your new neighbor, Ollie."

Emma tried to smile, but confusion and

embarrassment overwhelmed her.

"I'm sorry," Spencer said to Ollie. "She likes to make up stories."

"It's not a story," she said softly.

"Just clean up your mess, Emma."

She put the jars away and brushed the counter clean.

"Let's go home," Spencer said as she finished.

"But my elephant is in the other room. I can't just leave her. She needs her sandwiches."

"I'm on it," Ollie said with a wink.

"Thanks," Emma said. "Her name is Belaphant. Tell her I'm sorry I had to go."

"Belaphant the elephant," Ollie said, nodding. "I like it."

Emma smiled. She liked Ollie.

"See ya," Ollie said, waving to Spencer. And when the two had exited, he quickly glanced around, checking for signs of any tiny elephants. Then he smiled, lifted a sandwich to his lips, and devoured it in a few bites.

# 12

# No Such Thing as Magic

Neither Spencer nor Emma said much as they left the Johnson's home. But when they got back to their house, Spencer had plenty to say. "I can't believe you. You just blew it for us! Kids finally move in across the street, and you had to go wandering into their house, eating their food. Now they are going to think we're a couple of weirdos!"

"I'm sorry, Spencer. I didn't know. I didn't eat their food. I told you. My elephant was hungry."

"You don't just wander through someone's front door and—"

"I didn't."

"What?"

"I didn't go through the front door. I went through my closet."

Spencer let out a deep sigh. Then he closed his eyes and rubbed his forehead. "Emma, you can't just keep telling stories all the time."

"It's not a story, Spencer. Promise. Come on. I'll show you." And with that, she hurried up the stairs and down the hall to her bedroom.

Slowly Spencer followed, and there he found her standing next to her closet door.

"See for yourself," she said matter-of-factly.

"What? A messy closet? Your room is a disaster. If Mom sees this—"

"Uh! No Spencer," she said, hopping over things and kicking off her bunny slippers before jumping onto her bed so she could get a good view. "Go inside. You'll see."

Spencer sighed. He knew he shouldn't entertain her fantasies, but it seemed the only way to prove she was being ridiculous. He ducked under the hanging clothes and pushed his head inside. "There's nothing here," he said, his voice muffled by the stuff now covering his face.

"That's probably because half your body's still sticking out. You gotta go all the way in."

Inside the closet Spencer huffed, though Emma couldn't hear it. Then he took another step.

*Thunk!*

His head clonked hard against the back of the closet.

His face was flush and he looked even angrier when he came back out.

"It's not my fault!" Emma said. "Maybe—"

"Maybe nothing, Emma. It's just a closet! A stupid, messy closet."

"Mom said you're not allowed to say *stupid.* It's not nice."

"You know what's not nice? You ruining the chance for us to finally have kids to play with. You know what else? You living in an imaginary world when you're not a baby anymore. When are you going to grow up and realize there's no such thing as magic?"

Tears filled Emma's eyes. "Maybe you're just

jealous because you don't know how to do it."

Spencer turned away. "Whatever," he mumbled as he headed out the door and back to his room.

Emma ran to the door and closed it behind him. Turning back around, she took one look at the closet door and slammed it shut too. Then she ran to her bed and flopped face-first onto it.

# 13

## Big Brothers Don't Know Everything

Tears streamed from Emma's eyes and fell in large drops onto her pillow. She had always looked up to her brother. He knew things about the world, and she trusted him. But she just didn't want to believe him this time. Not about this. She didn't know how she ended up in the neighbor's home, and she felt badly now about helping herself to their food for her elephant. But she wasn't ready to see the world the way Spencer did. It was the same way her mom and dad did. And she had already seen him wear their same sad eyes.

* * *

Emma lay there for some time, her heart aching from Spencer's words. For a while, she hoped he would come back and apologize. But the more she thought about it, the more she realized that she really didn't want to be there if he did. She knew he wouldn't mean it. He would just say it because he felt bad. No, the truth was out. He thought she was a baby, and he didn't believe anything she said. Who needed him anyway? Her parents would be home in a few hours, and she could try to talk to them. Momma always listened. But she would be tired, and Emma had learned not to ask for too much when she came home like that. Besides, what would she be able to do? Make him take it back? It wouldn't matter anyway.

So Emma pulled her backpack from the corner and dumped the contents onto the bed. Then she stuffed in her blankey and a small bag of chips she had saved for an emergency. She zipped the bag shut, pulled it onto her shoulders, and slipped her feet back into her favorite bunny slippers. Then she took a deep breath, pulled open the closet door, and headed inside.

# 14

# The World Inside the Wall

Izzy was surprised to find that the space behind her bedroom wall was a lot bigger than she ever would have expected. Climbing inside, there was just room enough for a child to crawl. And Izzy did so, excited by the possibilities of what might be ahead. She decided too, that it was a good thing Ollie wasn't with her, as he'd be trying to talk her into going back, for fear of spiders or other creepy-crawly things that usually enjoy lurking in dark, undisturbed areas. But bugs and darkness didn't bother her. Quite the contrary, in fact. They were mysteries that excited her.

Apologizing to the spiders as she pushed their webs aside, Izzy crawled along, her flashlight showing the way. The space soon opened up, and Izzy found that she could stand with her fluffy pigtails just brushing the ceiling above her. The space was wider now too.

As she shined her flashlight around, it lit up something white on the floor ahead. At first, she thought it might be an animal. But as she approached, she found that it was, in fact, a pair of fluffy, white bunny slippers with a note attached: *Bunny Slippers Required Beyond this Point.*

Izzy felt exhilarated, and without hesitation she slipped them on. Just as her second foot was placed inside the perfectly-fitting slipper, a light went on down a long hall ahead. But now, as she flashed her light around, she could see that it was no longer the only hall. In fact, the space branched into many separate halls from here, all unlit, save for the one path directly ahead of her.

She was giddy at the possibilities, and wanted to explore them all. *But you must always start somewhere,* she reminded herself. "The hall seems to want me to go that way," she said aloud, shining her flashlight down the space that led to the light ahead. "And it hasn't disappointed me yet."

Her mind was made up. With one last look back at the faint light from her bedroom far down the hall behind her, Izzy headed down the hall in her new fluffy bunny slippers, in search of the mysterious light ahead.

# 15

# My House Ate My Sister

When Spencer got to Emma's room to apologize, the last thing he expected to find was her missing again. The closet door was open, and he peered at it suspiciously before searching its contents. But no Emma was there to be found.

He closed the door and continued to search the remainder of her room once more, which took all of a minute to toss through the things on the floor and look under the bed.

As though caught in a loop, he retraced his steps through the house to all her hiding places, then headed back outside. But no sooner had he walked around the house from the back to the front, when he saw Ollie running across the street.

"My sister's gone!" Ollie yelled.

His words took Spencer by surprise. *"Your* sister's missing?"

Ollie nodded frantically, his eyes wide.

"Mine is too," Spencer said, furrowing his brow as he attempted to contemplate the situation.

"Emma? Again? Are you sure?"

"I've searched everywhere." He turned to look from his house to Ollie's. "We had a fight. She was upset, but I really didn't expect she'd run off." His eyes were back on Ollie's house. "Do you think there's any chance they could be together?"

"I suppose, but I doubt it. I started hearing noises in my house shortly after you both left. I went to find Izzy to see if she was hearing any of it, but when I got to her room, she was gone."

Ollie looked nervously back at his house. "The thing is, when I saw her last, she was messing with some panel in her wall. And when I went back, the panel was open, and Izzy was gone."

"What was behind the panel?"

"No idea. I didn't look."

"Why not?"

"Well . . . you know . . . it was all dark and it's probably full of spiders."

"She's probably in there. It's the only logical explanation."

"But the bathroom's on the other side of the wall."

Spencer shrugged. "Then the space must be tight, and she could be stuck. We better check it out."

The idea of going back into the house still seemed to make Ollie nervous, but he waved Spencer on and the two headed back up his drive.

* * *

Inside the house, Ollie showed Spencer to Izzy's room. "See," he said as they passed the bathroom, "this room backs right up to it, so that space can't be more than a couple of inches deep."

The door to Izzy's room was open. Inside it was dark, save for a bit of sunlight filtering through the leaves of a large tree outside, into the window.

Ollie led the way into the small purple room and over to the panel at the base of the far left wall.

"What? No. This isn't right. It was open!" he said, trying to pull the panel aside. But it wouldn't move. "Great! My house ate my sister!"

"So now you *do* think she's inside?"

"I don't know. She's curious. And this house is creepy. So, who knows?"

Again and again, both boys tried pulling the panel this way and that, but it simply would not budge.

When at last they gave up, Ollie fell back onto his bottom, glaring at the mysterious panel. Spencer sat beside him, staring in frustrated confusion. Then he leaned forward and ran his fingers over the tiny crayon drawing of an elephant in the upper left corner. "What's this?"

"It's an elephant. The kid who lived here before must have drawn it." He paused to take a closer look. "But I swear it wasn't grinning earlier."

# 16

# More Bunny Slippers

"I don't get it," Spencer said. "Earlier my sister was going on about something in her closet, and now this. There has to be a connection."

"As far as I know, they haven't even met yet," Ollie said.

Spencer shook his head. "It doesn't make any logical sense." He pressed a hand against his forehead. Then he began to retell the story of his fight with Emma and how she claimed something was going on inside her closet.

When at last he had finished, Ollie said, "Maybe both houses are haunted?"

"They say the whole street is supposed to be

haunted, but that's just a story. There has to be a logical explanation. I think we should take another look at Emma's closet."

"Are you sure? What if something happens to us too?"

"At least we won't be in trouble for losing our sisters."

"Good point. Let's go."

So the two boys headed back to Spencer's house, and this time Spencer showed Ollie upstairs to Emma's room.

"Whoa," he said when they stepped in and Ollie got a look at the clothes and toys scattered everywhere. "And I thought my room was messy."

Spencer frowned. "She claims the elephant did it."

Ollie laughed. Unlike Spencer, Ollie rather enjoyed Emma's playful imagination. "I take it she likes pink," he said, tossing things aside so he wouldn't step on them. He stopped in front of the door on the right hand wall. "Is this the closet?"

Spencer stepped beside him, grabbed the handle, and he threw open the door.

Ollie gave a little gasp. He had expected to see something strange or wonderful inside, but instead, it was just a normal, everyday closet. A little messy, and filled with more pink clothes than he had ever seen in one place, but a regular closet nonetheless. That is, save for the two pairs of bunny slippers sitting directly inside the door with their toes pointed towards the back of the closet.

"Your sister got a thing for bunny slippers?" Ollie asked.

Spencer eyed them suspiciously. "These weren't here earlier. And they're much too big for Emma. In fact, they're—" his words broke off as he reached down, took a slipper, and matched it up to his own foot. "My size."

His eyes met Ollie's. "Emma was wearing ones just like it earlier."

Ollie moved a foot so it rested beside the second set of slippers. "A perfect fit, it appears." His eyes met Spencer's once more. "I think you know what this means."

# 17

# Watch Your Head

"I don't understand what a pair of slippers could have to do with Emma's disappearance," Spencer said as he watched Ollie step out of his shoes and into the slippers.

"I don't yet either, but it's the only clue we've got," he said, looking down to admire the fuzzy faces below. Ollie grinned. "They're actually quite comfy." He hopped up and down in them. "Yeah, I could get used to this," he said, doing a little dance.

Spencer rubbed hard at his forehead. "But how does it help us find our sisters?"

Ollie stopped suddenly. "Right, sorry," he

said, grinning sheepishly. And he turned to face the closet once more. "You said she claimed she went into the closet and came out at my house. So maybe they're connected somehow, and these slippers are like a key or something?"

Ollie appeared to be serious, and Spencer was beginning to think he might have gotten further finding his sister on his own. "No offense, but that's the most ridiculous idea I've ever heard."

"You got any better ideas?"

Unfortunately, Spencer did not.

"Okay, well, my sister's way into science, and she's always saying that the best way of figuring something out is to come up with an idea and then test it. So I have a theory that these slippers and this closet are the key to finding our sisters, and I'm gonna test it out."

He glanced back at Spencer, who held an expression that said: You. Are. Crazy.

So Ollie said, "Hey, it's just an idea, right? It may not work. But if it does—"

"Okay. How are you going to test this idea?"

"I'm going in," Ollie said, pointing to the

back of the closet.

Spencer sighed, then waved a hand towards the closet. “Be my guest. But watch your head.”

“Will do.”

And with that, Ollie pushed the hanging clothes aside, stepped into the closet, and disappeared.

# 18

## The Joke's on Me

The hanging clothes shifted back into place, obscuring any sight of Ollie. Spencer expected to hear him clonk the back of the closet seconds later. But he didn't.

He expected to hear Ollie's muffled voice as he rummaged through the clothes and junk on the floor.

But he didn't.

He expected to see Ollie's head emerge from the pink clothes any second now. But it didn't.

So Spencer began to call, "See anything?"

No answer came.

"Ollie, what are you doing?"

No answer.

And finally, "Ollie, where are you? Come on, Ollie!"

But, again, Ollie didn't answer.

Spencer kicked the other pair of bunny slippers aside. The light filtering in through the bedroom window was just enough for him to make out the back of the closet as he pushed away the hanging clothes. He stepped inside and felt around until he found either end of the small closet space. He expected to run into Ollie. But he didn't.

"What the?" he said aloud, the hanging clothes flumping against his face as he stepped back out of the closet. "This doesn't make any logical sense!"

He was getting angry now. His sister was gone. His neighbor's sister was gone. And now, the only friend he had made in a long while was now gone too.

Maybe he hadn't been watching closely, and Ollie had slipped out of the bedroom door? Maybe it was all a big trick organized by Emma to make Spencer look ridiculous in front of the new neighbors?

Furious, Spencer flung open the bedroom door and stomped through the house. "This isn't funny Emma! I know you're here! I'm not playing your stupid games!"

But Emma didn't giggle. She, Izzy, and Ollie didn't jump out laughing at what a great prank it was. Instead, his shouts were met by utter silence.

# 19

# Into the Closet

Spencer flopped down onto the old living room sofa to think. Where could they all be? Had Ollie left the room and they had all run off back to his house? But he didn't see Ollie leave.

*My sister says to solve a problem you have to come up with a theory and test it,* Ollie had said. Spencer needed a theory. But all he could think of was Ollie putting those slippers on and stepping into the closet.

*I can't do it,* Spencer thought. *It's too ridiculous. I'm not wearing bunny slippers!*

He looked up at the clock on the mantle

above the fireplace. Time was quickly ticking by. His parents would be home in a couple of hours, and Spencer would have to explain where Emma was.

*No. I'm not, under any circumstances putting on bunny slippers,* he tried to convince himself.

He sat and waited, arms crossed.

*Tick* went the clock.

*Tick.*

*Tick.*

*Tick.*

He looked at the clock again.

*Tick.*

*Tick.*

*Tick.*

He sighed loudly.

*Tick.*

*Tick.*

Spencer grunted angrily. He had no choice. Silly or not. He had to try it.

Reluctantly, he returned to Emma's room. He still half-expected the group to jump out and surprise him, laughing at the joke as he walked back in, but the house was still silent.

He huffed in frustration as he slipped the bunny slippers on. He didn't want to wear silly bunnies on his feet. Even if they were comfortable.

He didn't feel anything special as he slipped them on. No magical tingle came over him. No second sight or x-ray vision or heightened senses. All he felt was confident that it was all a waste of time. But he was out of ideas. He turned to face the closet once more, pushed the hanging clothes aside, and stepped inside, squinching his eyes shut as he fully expected to smack into the back of the closet.

But he didn't.

He reached forward and his fingers reached into nothingness.

His heart began to race. *Where was the wall? He couldn't find the wall!*

Cautiously, Spencer stepped forward. But suddenly the floor disappeared! He began screaming and falling—

down,

down,

down,

down,
until—

*Plumf!*

# 20

# A World of White

Spencer had crashed face-down into what felt like a massive feather pillow.

"It's about time," Ollie said.

"Dude, why didn't you take the slide?"

"Clearly there wasn't a slide," Spencer said, his voice muffled by the fluffiness his face was smashed into. It was soft beneath his body, and the fall into the giant cushion might have even been pleasant if he hadn't been so terrified.

Spencer pressed a hand into the pillow and lifted his face from it, then turned to see Ollie's head, peeking over the top of the pillow. He was grinning happily.

"I mean, the pillow jump looked like a lot of fun too," Ollie said, "but the slide was amazing!"

Spencer couldn't understand how it was that Ollie seemed to be having fun under these circumstances. He pressed his other hand into the fluffiness and pushed himself into a seated position. The cushion was so soft that when he sank down into it, it rose up half a foot around him on all sides. He sat there for a moment, trying to figure out how to get up, for if he tried to stand, he'd surely fall right back down into the pillow. So he got onto his hands and knees and slowly crawled towards Ollie. But with each movement forward, he sunk into the pillow, making the journey difficult. He fell on his face several times and felt frustrated and embarrassed by the time he reached Ollie. At last, he reached up, grabbed Ollie's hands, and held on tight as Ollie tugged him free.

Spencer was relieved when his feet hit the floor. "Thanks," he said, truly appreciative for Ollie's help.

"Anytime," Ollie said, still smiling.

Spencer looked back at him, still trying to figure Ollie out. He was different, but kind. And he didn't make Spencer nervous or uncomfortable the way Spencer often felt with other kids his age.

"So where are we?" Spencer asked.

"No idea. I looked around a bit before you came down, but there doesn't seem to be anything here," he said, turning in circles to view a vast white emptiness. "I've never seen anything like it."

Spencer gazed around the room in awe. They were clearly standing somewhere, but it appeared to be more like nowhere. Everything around them was white, just like the large pillow he had fallen into. The pillow took up more than half the room, but there was nothing else there, aside from the four white walls that surrounded them.

Spencer's brow furrowed, his fists now on his hips. "Well clearly the girls aren't here, so this was a big mistake."

"I don't know, aren't you even a little bit curious about what this place is?"

"Ollie, we have to find our sisters. How do we get out?"

Ollie shrugged. "Beats me."

"Wait, didn't you say you came down a slide?"

"Oh yeah. Incredible. So many twists and turns! Best one ev—"

"Where is it?"

"Huh?"

"The slide. There's no slide."

"Yeah, well, I had turned my back to look around," Ollie said, spinning around to demonstrate.

Spencer turned too, following Ollie's lead.

"And when I heard you screaming, I turned back around. That's when I saw that the slide had been replaced by a giant pillow." He turned back to gesture at the pillow, but it was now gone, along with the door high overhead. "Huh," Ollie said. "Well, will you look at that?"

"We're trapped!" Spencer yelled. "I can't believe it! My parents will be home any time now, Emma's missing, and we're—" His eyes darted about, trying to understand. "Lost in a room that shouldn't even be here!"

The sound of his voice trailed off, echoing through the empty room.

"Maybe we just have to turn around again?" Ollie said. He turned to look across the room and spun back again.

But no exit appeared. The room was bare, and the two were alone, save for the four blank white walls.

# 21

# The Impossible

"HELP!" Spencer called into the nothingness. "ANYONE! WE'RE DOWN HERE!"

"I kinda doubt anyone is going to find us," Ollie said. "Our houses are the only ones on the street, and none of our parents are home. And even if they were, I doubt they'd think to put on bunny slippers and walk into the closet."

Spencer was trying to hold back tears. He had failed. His parents had trusted him to be grown up and responsible, to keep the house in order, and keep him and Emma safe until they arrived home. But he had failed. And now he and Emma were both lost. Probably forever.

His legs felt weak, and he let them collapse beneath him as he sat down on the floor.

"I just don't understand," he said after a long pause. "There was never a room inside Emma's closet before. And it's too big to be a room no one knew about. If my parents knew about it, they would have told us. We could have used it as a playroom or something. This place makes no sense. None of this is even possible. This place doesn't exist."

"I—uh—hate to disagree," Ollie said, "but I think it's safe to say that it does."

"But they were all just *stories*. Silly stories for children."

Ollie raised an eyebrow. "What stories?" He stepped closer and sat down cross-legged on the floor across from Spencer. "Does this have to do with . . . with the . . . *ghosts?*"

"No. Maybe. I don't know."

"I think you better tell me."

Spencer inhaled deeply. "We moved here when I was really little. There were people in your house at the time, but they were moving out. On the last day, as they were packing up the van to go, the boy—much older than I was—came over and asked for me." Spencer looked up at Ollie, meeting his eyes. "He had never talked to me before." His eyes moved away as he recalled the old memory. "He said the street didn't used to end with our houses."

"It wasn't a dead end?"

"Nope. It continued on and on. But one day, it just disappeared."

"Lost Lane," Ollie said softly.

Spencer nodded. "I didn't know what to think at the time. And I had so many questions afterward. But the family left and I never saw him again, and the house has been empty ever since. Until now."

"Whoa."

"With time, I decided it was just a story the kid made up to mess with me before he left."

"Maybe not," Ollie said.

"But it's not possible. There has to be a logical explanation. This is probably just a secret basement room someone created."

"With a disappearing slide and giant feather pillow? Where the only way to gain access is by wearing bunny slippers in your size that somehow appear when you need them? I don't think so."

"Then what?"

"It's gotta be magic."

"I don't believe in magic."

"Maybe that's the problem."

Ollie's words cut through Spencer. "You think it's my fault we're stuck here?"

"I didn't say that. But I do think we need to keep an open mind so we can imagine a way out."

"But I don't understand how that would—" Spencer's eye caught something strange, and he quickly got up and moved across the room. "I don't remember seeing this before."

Ollie got up quickly and met Spencer on the other side of the room. Sure enough, a pile of items now lay on the floor. He stared at it a long while before tilting his head up to gaze at the space above them. "Spencer! Look! There's a door!"

# 22

# A Bouncing Breakthrough

It was a strange assortment of items that lay in a heap on the stark white floor. A large piece of rubber, a set of screws and other hardware, several poles, and some strange stretchy cord with hooks that Ollie couldn't quite make sense of. "Maybe we can build a ladder?" he said, sifting excitedly through the items and tossing aside those that didn't seem like they would work.

Spencer watched, staring at each item intently. He looked back and forth several times from the pile to the opening far overhead, his left fist pressed against his mouth as he thought.

"No, I don't think it's a ladder," he said at last. "But we could build a trampoline."

Ollie looked up at him, surprised. "You sure?"

Spencer reached down and began pulling pieces into a new pile. "Yeah. See these poles will fit together with this hardware to build a frame, and then these bungee cords will attach the large piece of rubber to the frame. It'll be super springy. We should be able to bounce up to the opening."

Ollie grinned. "Dude, that's amazing!"

"What?"

"You figured that out, just like that. That's incredible!"

Spencer blushed, but didn't say another word. Instead he went straight to work.

"What can I do?" Ollie asked, jumping to his side.

Spencer explained to him how to join the poles using the twist-on joints, screws, and wing nuts provided.

Working together, they had the frame up in no time. Then they quickly moved on to attaching the rubber top.

"Now be careful with these," Spencer warned as they attached the first cords. "If you stretch it out and it doesn't hook right, it'll snap back and do some real damage."

"Good warning. I'll be extra careful."

And he was.

Soon the trampoline was ready to go, and the two boys stood back to admire their work. Then Ollie stepped forward and gave it a good shake just to be sure. The frame stood solid. "We did it!" he said proudly. "I can't believe it. And there isn't a single piece left over. How did you figure that out so easily?"

Spencer was blushing again, and he shrugged shyly. "I don't know. I just really like building things."

Ollie smiled, turning back to admire their creation once more. "I can see why."

"Well," Spencer said, "I guess there's only one thing left to do. It's time we try it. Ever jumped on a trampoline before?"

Ollie shook his head.

"Me neither. But I'm pretty sure it'll take us

where we need to go." He looked at the door determinedly. "Mind if I give it the first try?"

"It's your creation. Be my guest."

"Let's push it into the corner first," Spencer said. "That will give it more stability as well as protection on two sides, and it should position us so we can jump right up into that doorway."

So each boy took a side, and together they pushed it into the corner so that one side lay directly below the doorway above. Then Spencer grabbed onto a side and pulled himself up onto the trampoline.

As he rolled onto its top, all his fear and anxiety melted away. And as he stood, Ollie saw something he had not yet seen: Spencer smiled. He couldn't help it. Not only was it one of the largest and most exciting things he had ever built, but it was bouncy and boingy under his feet.

Excitement and anticipation rushed through him as he bent his knees low and took his first jump.

*Bounce.*

"Ha!"

*Bounce, bounce.*

"Hahahaha!"

*Bounce, bounce, bounce.* The ears of his bunny slippers flopped about on his feet, but Spencer was laughing so hard now, he didn't even notice.

*Bounce, bounce, bounce, bounce.* "Woo hooo!" he cried, his entire face alight in glee.

*Bounce, bounce, bounce, bounce, bounce.* Each jump was a little higher than the last.

*Bounce, bounce, bounce, bounce, bounce, bounce.* Spencer hadn't had this much fun in years!

*Bounce, bounce, bounce, bounce, bounce, bounce, bounce.* Higher and higher he went, calling out in happiness as Ollie cheered him on.

*Bounce, bounce, bounce.* He was parallel with the door!

*Bounce, bounce, bounce.* He reached out and grabbed for the handle. Missed!

*Bounce, Bounce, Bounce, BOING!* He grabbed it again. Success!

The door flew open and bright light shown

in.

Ollie cheered louder from far below. "You're doing it! Great job! Now jump inside!"

*Bounce, Bounce, Bounce,*

BOUNCE!

Spencer flung himself forward and landed face-first on the floor above with his legs dangling out. But he was smiling and laughing as he pulled himself to his feet.

He felt exhilarated like never before as he looked down and saw that Ollie had already climbed onto the trampoline and was bouncing happily away.

# 23

## The Primary Situation

The two boys were having so much fun, in fact, that it wasn't until after Spencer had helped pull Ollie into the room that he finally got a good look around. Then the smiles quickly faded from their faces.

Spencer hadn't really thought about where the new door would lead, but if he had thought about it, he might have guessed it'd take them back into Emma's closet. But it didn't.

In fact, at first glance, the new room appeared very much like the last: large, white, and empty. But then—wait, what was that far across the room?

"Ollie? Is that you?" a voice called.

Ollie recognized it at once. "Come on, Spencer!" he called as he took off running.

But Spencer hesitated, turning back to take one more look at the door they had entered through. But it had already disappeared.

At the far end of the room, Spencer caught up with Ollie. They appeared to now be in some sort of laboratory.

Through a cloud of white sweet-smelling smoke, Ollie could just barely make out the outline of pom-pom pigtails behind a table of beakers, burners, and microscopes. "Izzy?"

She rounded the lab table, and he could now see that her glasses were covered in large goggles. She wore a white lab coat speckled in purple splotches. "Ollie, great!" she said, hurrying over to him. She appeared so excited to see her brother she didn't even seem to notice Spencer standing there. "You gotta see this," she said, taking his hand and pulling him to the other side of the table. "I've made a new kind of soft drink. I call it Purple Pow. It's fizzy and makes you burp purple bubbles."

"Why?" Spencer interjected.

Izzy turned and looked at him quizzically. "Because it's fun."

"This is Spencer," Ollie said, gesturing to his new friend.

"I'm Izzy," she said. "You like science?"

"I'm more into building things."

"Bummer. Well, I can show you the new lab anyway," but when she turned back, the lab and all its equipment had vanished. "Oh no!" she called, running to where her experiments had been. "Where did it go?"

"Who knows," Ollie replied. "The same thing keeps happening to us. Things show up, then they disappear. This place is unpredictable."

Izzy sighed. "Hmm . . ." she said, considering this. "Maybe it's not unpredictable? Maybe we just don't know how to predict it yet? We need to explore it further. Maybe run some tests."

Spencer shook his head. "We don't have time for that right now. We have to find my sister. You haven't seen a little girl in pigtails around here have you?"

Izzy shook her head. "Sorry."

So Ollie briefly caught Izzy up on the events she had missed, from Emma appearing at their house claiming to be gathering food for a small elephant, to him and Spencer putting on the slippers and taking their own paths from the closet to the white room.

Izzy smiled, her eyes wide through the entire story. She couldn't help but keep interjecting comments and questions. "So putting on the slippers activates some kind of magic gateway," she said excitedly.

"Yeah, and I figured that one out! Who's the scientist now?" he said, grinning.

Izzy gave him a high five. "Nicely done!"

Spencer watched them jealously. It had been a while since he and Emma had gotten along this well. It was before his parents both worked so much, and one of them would be home with them before and after school. But as they grew older, money got tighter, and Mom and Dad trusted Spencer to help hold things together for them while they were away at work. Spencer knew then that he had to put away his childish ways. He was responsible for taking care of himself and Emma and the house when they weren't home. And that meant thinking and acting like a grownup. He liked that they trusted him. But deep down, he missed the care-free days of playing make-believe and other games with his sister. And they had grown apart more each day since.

"So you haven't actually tried to leave here yet?" Spencer asked.

"No, I, uh, well there was lab equipment." Izzy stopped and smiled. "I've never had access to such great equipment. It never even occurred to me to leave. Now that you mention it though, I am getting hungry. You didn't bring any food, did you?"

The boys shook their heads.

"Bummer. Well, the panel in my room led to a passage with these slippers. I put them on and followed along until it opened into a hallway that led to this room. But, as you can see," she said, motioning to a solid, empty wall across the room, "the hallway's now gone. So I guess we'll just have to find a new way out."

"Now then," she said, walking across the

room to the space that had been left in the wake of her former laboratory. "What do we have here?"

And sure enough, there were now lamps—three of them—one attached to each of three walls. One contained a red light, one blue, and one yellow. The fourth wall was empty and white.

"Three lights, all primary colors," Izzy said, walking over to the red light.

Spencer headed over to examine the yellow light. It swiveled this way and that, and he moved the lamp head to one side so he could examine how it was mounted to the wall. "If we can find some tools, I think I can get it off the wall so we can take it apart. Then maybe we can use the parts to build something to help us get out of here."

"I don't think that's going to work," Izzy said. "I think it's attached there for a reason."

Ollie pulled hard at the blue light. Like the yellow, it swiveled about, but it didn't budge from the wall. "Yeah, I don't think it's coming off." He released the light and twirled about to view the ceiling above. "Besides, there's no door to reach."

"He's right," Spencer said, shining the yellow light around to get a better look. "There's no door here."

But as he shined it around, his yellow beam crossed Izzy's red one. "Stop Spencer!" she said suddenly.

"Ooo! Cool!" Ollie said, admiring the orange light that was formed when the two beams crossed.

Izzy's face shone with excitement. "Maybe that's it? Maybe we have to cross the lights to access a gateway? Everyone, shine your light in the center of the blank wall!"

So with each child on their own light, the three kids swiveled their beams until they crossed at the center of the fourth, white wall. Izzy was certain the trick would work, but no door appeared. Yet, she seemed unfazed. "Okay, that didn't work, but I think we're on to something."

"Maybe we just need to dance them around on the wall?" Ollie said, messing around as he swizzled and flashed blue light across the wall. Izzy laughed and swirled hers about too. And just as the two beams crossed, a beautiful purple light appeared.

"That's it!" Izzy cried. "Spencer, shine your beam on Ollie's!"

And sure enough, just as he did, something amazing happened. A tiny door appeared just inside the overlapping circle of green light.

"Of course," Izzy said. "Yellow plus blue makes green. Green means go!"

"But it's too small," Ollie said. "We'll never fit through that door."

"Maybe they adjust," Izzy said, playing with the knobs on her lamp. And sure enough, as she turned a knob, the size of her beam grew even smaller.

"The other way, Izzy," Ollie said, watching as the beam and door shrank on the wall.

As Izzy turned the other way, Spencer found the knob on his own lamp, and together the two circles of light on the opposite wall grew along with the door inside them. The door now sat right along the floor on the far wall, but it was still not quite large enough for them to fit through, as Ollie demonstrated now standing next to it.

"That's as far as the knob goes," Spencer said.

"We need to increase the distance," Izzy said. "Spencer, let's try shining our lights higher up. It'll increase the angle, thereby increasing the size of the overall circle of light on the wall."

Sure enough, it was just enough to do the trick, but the bottom of the doorway was now above Ollie's head.

"That's the best we can do," Izzy said, leaving her light fixed in its position and walking across the room to examine the door cast in green light. "We're just gonna have to find a way to get in there."

# 24

## Team Building

"Izzy, climb on my back," Ollie said, bending down. Izzy climbed on, but it was quickly apparent that she was nowhere near tall enough to reach the door handle high above her head. So Ollie lowered her back down, saying, "Try my shoulders."

"Are you sure?" she said, looking nervous.

Ollie nodded and knelt down on the floor. "It's the only way."

"I'll help make sure you don't fall off," Spencer assured her.

"You know, accidents are the leading cause of death," she said pushing her glasses further up her nose. Spencer frowned, and reluctantly, Izzy climbed onto her brother's shoulders.

Ollie struggled to get back up off his knees. But a moment later, he was up.

And while Ollie wobbled as he tried to keep her upright, Spencer did just as he said, reaching up to steady Izzy as she leaned from one side to the next, and guiding her upright when she fell too far this way or that.

But despite their efforts, Izzy was not yet high enough to reach the door handle, which remained just out of reach.

Still holding up his hands to catch her if needed, Spencer glanced back around the room looking for other resources to help them. But the three lights were the only equipment in the room, and he didn't dare touch them now and risk the doorway disappearing again.

Izzy continued to stretch and reach for the knob.

Then suddenly, she lost her balance!

"WHOOOOA!!!" she called as she fell forward hard into the door.

But to her surprise, it pushed open, and she

tumbled inside.

Ollie called after her. "Are you okay?"

Inside the doorway, Izzy pulled herself to her feet, turned, and smiled. "Yeah, I'm fine. That was a happy accident, huh?" she said, looking down at them several feet below. Now we just have to figure out how to get you two up here."

Spencer knelt down on one knee. "Step here," he said to Ollie, gesturing to his knee. "See if you can reach the opening."

Izzy was now flat on the floor overhead, her head and arms dangling out the doorway, reaching out to her brother. "Come on, Ollie, I'm ready!"

"Wait, how tall are you?" Ollie asked Spencer.

Spencer shrugged. "I don't know."

"Stand up a minute." Ollie turned back to his sister. "Hey Izzy, who's taller?" he called as he turned back to back with Spencer.

"You are, by just a bit," Izzy called back.

"Maybe you should go next then?" Ollie said. "It seems like we should probably leave the tallest to go last."

Spencer shrugged. "Yeah, I guess that seems

logical."

So Ollie knelt down just as Spencer had done moments earlier, and Spencer stepped up onto his thigh.

Ollie gave a painful yelp.

"You okay?" Spencer called back.

"Yeah, fine," he said through gritted teeth. "Izzy, you got him?"

"Almost!" she called back. "A little further, Spencer! Gotcha! Wait. Don't pull so hard!"

"I'm not trying to!" Spencer said, but he and Izzy were both slipping as his weight began slowly pulling her from the doorway above.

"Hang on!" Ollie called, getting quickly to his feet. He grabbed Spencer around the legs and hoisted him up. Izzy slid back into the room above as Spencer reached up, grabbed the door frame, and pulled himself inside.

Ollie danced around on the floor below, both in celebration of their victory, and to distract himself from the fact that he was now alone in the room. But Izzy and Spencer both quickly appeared back in the doorway.

"Okay," Izzy said. "Now we just need to

find a way to get you up here," she said to her brother below.

"I'm thinking a running jump," Ollie said.

Izzy got quickly back into position on the floor. "I'll pull you up, Ollie."

"How about I help make sure he doesn't pull you down with him?" Spencer said to Izzy. "How about locking your feet on the inside of the doorway, and I'll hold onto your ankles to make sure you don't fall."

"Yes, please," Izzy called, face already out the door and arms reaching out for her brother. She locked her feet as Spencer had said, and he grabbed her ankles and held them tightly.

"Okay, Ollie!" Izzy called. Give it a big running jump!"

Down below, Ollie had danced back across the room and was now dancing back and forth to get himself ready. Then he took off running and leapt into the air.

Missed.

"Ah, so close!" Spencer said.

For a split second, the blue light flickered. And in that second, Ollie saw the door vanish, along with his sister.

Ollie let out a scream.

Then the blue light flicked back on, and the doorway and Izzy returned.

"What's wrong, Ollie?" Izzy said.

His face looked like he had seen a ghost. "Where did you go?"

"Nowhere. I've been right here."

"I've been hanging onto her the whole time," Spencer called from inside the next room.

"No you weren't. The blue light went out and you and the door were gone!

"Oh no!" Izzy yelled. "The lights are losing power. We are running out of time!"

Spencer watched the yellow light start to waver. "Hurry Ollie!" he called.

Ollie jogged to the far side of the room.

He ran faster this time.

Jumped.

Missed again!

"Try again, Ollie, quickly!" Izzy yelled as Ollie headed back into position.

He started to hum a little tune as he danced around. Then he stopped, stared at his goal, and said, "I just need to relax. I got this."

He took off running again.

He leapt up as far he could, with both hands high in the air.

Izzy's hands locked tightly with his!

"I GOT HIM! PULL ME UP, SPENCER!" Izzy called.

Spencer leaned back and pulled with all his might.

"WOOOOAHHH!" Izzy called again as her belly scooted slowly backward along the floor. "IT'S WORKING!" she called. Izzy was now fully back inside the room with Spencer again, but Ollie still dangled from her hands. "HOLD ON OLLIE!" she called. "JUST A LITTLE FARTHER, SPENCER!"

But Spencer was growing very tired. He struggled against it and pulled some more.

"I ALMOST GOT IT!" he heard Ollie shout.

Doubt was beginning to creep into Spencer's mind. His arms were aching with exhaustion, crying out for him to let go. But there was too much at stake. He couldn't let Ollie fall.

He closed his eyes, then grunted loudly as he pulled once more.

"GOT IT!" Ollie cried. He had reached the doorway!

Relief washed over Spencer as he released his hold on Izzy's ankles.

Izzy quickly scrambled to her feet.

Ollie was now almost halfway into the room and was struggling against the door frame, trying to pull himself in. Spencer and Izzy each reached down a hand and helped him the rest of the way.

Just as Ollie's feet touched the floor of the new room, the three colored lights in room below went out. And with it, the door they had just gone through vanished.

"We did it!" Izzy squealed.

"Nice work, Spencer!" Ollie said, smiling as he held up his hand for a high-five.

Spencer had never given a high-five before. Before today he had always felt it was a little silly. But now he smiled and clapped Ollie's hand proudly.

# 25

## Ollie's Room

As they turned to explore their new surroundings, lights turned on around them, illuminating another plain, white space.

Disappointment washed over Spencer. "I don't understand. How many of these rooms are there? We don't seem to be getting anywhere."

"We don't know that," Izzy said. "We just haven't figured out how it all works yet. Besides, how do we even know this is a different room?"

Spencer was now truly confused. "What do you mean?"

"It sure doesn't look any different from the last. What if somehow it's the same room that keeps putting us through test after test?"

Spencer tried to respond, but no words came. He simply couldn't wrap his mind around the events of the day so far, let alone the idea of a room that wouldn't let them go. "So we're trapped," he said at last.

"Not necessarily," Izzy replied.

"I think it has something to do with Lost Lane," Ollie interjected. "Maybe all these rooms were in those houses you said disappeared."

"What houses?" Izzy said. "No one told me about missing houses."

So while Spencer continued to scan the room for any way to escape, Ollie quickly filled Izzy in on everything Spencer had told him earlier.

"Fascinating!" Izzy replied. "Oh, I love our new house!"

The boys shared looks of utter disbelief.

"What?" she said innocently.

Rubbing his forehead in a manner he had seen his father do many times, Spencer said, "I just want to know why everything keeps changing and disappearing on us? Why is there no exit? And where's Emma? Why haven't we found her yet?"

"I think it's a puzzle," Izzy said. "And if we solve it, we'll find her."

"But *why* is it a puzzle? I just wanna know why it's here," he replied.

Izzy could see he was quite upset. Her eyes darted to her brother, who stood by quietly. "I don't know," she answered. "But I'm sure we can figure it out together."

Spencer sighed, but his eyes met Izzy's and then Ollie's. Then to Izzy's surprise, he slowly nodded.

Izzy smiled. Then she turned and walked over to examine the next wall.

*Tap.*

*Tap.*

*Tap.*

*Tap.*

She stopped abruptly to stare at the furry, floppy-eared faces on her feet.

Ollie quickly lifted a foot to examine a slipper of his own. His face lit up. "Oh yeah!" he said, seeing the metal taps that were now attached. He jumped up and down, then began to tap away.

Spencer and Izzy were still trying to understand this new turn of events when Ollie stopped again suddenly. "Oh! I get it!" he said, his face alight with glee. But he said no more and went right on dancing.

Spencer and Izzy exchanged glances. Then Izzy said, "Ollie, you're an amazing dancer. But really, this isn't the time. We need to figure out what this room's puzzle might be."

Ollie smiled but kept on dancing. "I'm working on it right now. Don't you get it?"

Spencer and Izzy traded confused looks once more.

"Spencer loves to design and build," Ollie said. "Our first puzzle was just for him. It gave him the tools, and he had to engineer a way out of there for us.

"The second one was for you. You knew the science behind which colors and angles would work to create a door large enough for us to escape.

"And this one," he said, still tapping around like it was his best day, "this room is all mine."

Izzy looked at him proudly. "Of course! Excellent, Ollie! Except . . . where's the door?"

"I can't believe I'm saying this, but he's right," Spencer said. "But he forgot something. It didn't take just one person to get us out of each room. We each had to work together in order to make it work."

Ollie looked happier than ever. "I've always wanted to be part of a dancing team!"

Normally, Izzy wasn't much for dancing, but now her curiosity overtook her. Could their dancing together open another door? There was only one way to find out. *Tap, tap, tappity tap. Tappity, tappity, tappity tap.* Giggles rolled out of her. "Hey, this is actually kinda fun!"

"See? I've been trying to tell you that for years!"

The two laughed together as they danced along happily.

"Come on, Spencer!" Ollie said.

Spencer looked at the floppy faces at his feet. Then he looked back up at his neighbors dancing away. "I—uh, I can't dance."

"Nonsense!" Ollie called back as he tapped

across the floor. "Just move about and let the taps do the rest. Find a beat and move with it."

Spencer wasn't so sure. He had never really tried to dance before, but he also really didn't know what he was doing. He felt like there must be some method to it, for which he had never been given any instruction. Nonetheless, despite the two now dancing away around the room, there was no door yet to be seen. And he knew time had to be getting short. His parents would be home soon. And who knew if Emma was in danger?

*Tap.* The ears on his bunny slippers flopped up and down.

*Tap tap.* They flopped some more.

*Tap tap tap-tap-tap.* Again and again they flipped and flopped, and Spencer couldn't help but laugh out loud. "This is the most ridiculous thing I have ever done," he said, now smiling as he tapped his feet.

"It's working!" Ollie cried. "Look!"

And sure enough, the faint outline of a door had begun to appear.

"Keep going everyone!" Izzy called. "We're

doing it!"

*Tap-tap-tappity-tap-tappity-tap. Tappity-tappity-tappity-tappity-tap.* Bunny ears were flapping and flopping all over the place, and Spencer was laughing along with Izzy and Ollie as they waved their arms about, dancing like they had been doing it together for years.

"You know this doesn't make any logical sense!" Spencer called to Ollie above the tapping.

Ollie grinned and just kept on dancing. "Yeah, but it sure is a whole lot of fun!"

The door was becoming more defined with each tap, and soon it looked as though it were almost solid.

"Everyone, dance on over to the door so we can jump out when it's time," Izzy said, moving in that direction. And the two boys followed.

When at last the door came into full focus, Izzy reached out, grabbed the handle, and pushed the door open. "We're gonna have to be quick," she said. "It's likely to disappear as soon as we stop dancing." The boys nodded as they continued tapping. "Okay, get close. Here we go. One . . . Two . . . Three!"

Izzy jumped through, Ollie followed, and Spencer could see they were both safely through. But as his feet left the floor, he saw the door quickly fade. And instead of finding himself safely on the other side, he smacked into a blank, white wall.

# 26

## The Path to Emma

"NOOOOO!!!!!" Spencer shouted, pounding on the wall where the door had just been.

He started to dance again, but the taps were now gone from his slippers.

"Noooooo," he said again, finally turning his back to the wall. His voice echoed through the empty room.

He stood there a long time. Then slowly his body crumpled to the floor in a defeated heap.

* * *

Spencer wasn't sure how long he had been sitting there. He felt sad and angry, like somehow the room had it out for him from the start.

It must be about time for his parents to be home now. He imagined Ollie and Izzy finding Emma and taking her back to his house, returning her safely to his parents. Of course, they wouldn't be able to explain where he had gone, so they'd have to say they didn't know. And it'd appear he'd run off, unable to handle something as simple as taking care of his little sister.

But then, what if they didn't find Emma? Who knew where she might be now? Maybe there were more rooms, and maybe she was trapped somewhere beyond here? Fear washed over him. He had to find his sister.

He padded through the room, the long ears of his slippered feet flopping up and down with each step. But Spencer didn't notice.

He examined the far wall, then the one next to it, checking for any hidden panels or clues he might have missed. Then he stood back and took a long look at the ceiling. It was far overhead, without any sign it could be reached without assistance.

So he stopped to ponder all he had experienced the last few hours, searching for patterns, trying to make sense of it all.

The bunny slippers were required to enter the space. Even Izzy had found that, and Spencer was sure it was how Emma had disappeared too.

When Ollie entered the first room, he came via slide. Spencer by falling. Then they were trapped. But Izzy hadn't been trapped—not that she knew of—not until the boys arrived. She had found lab equipment, and for her the discovery was like a dream come true. Ollie had said that he loved the slide. But Spencer fell and had been frightened by the idea of being trapped and locked away from finding his sister.

All along, Ollie and Izzy seemed to be enjoying themselves. But Spencer had been finding the experience much more difficult. But then, he thought, it hadn't been all bad. He had actually enjoyed making the trampoline, not to mention bouncing on it. And it felt pretty good when they pulled Ollie up through the green door in the second room. And he had to admit that it really was fun tap dancing along with Izzy and Ollie.

But he couldn't help but think that the room had kept him behind on purpose. All along it seemed to give them what they wanted or needed most, or maybe what they expected to find. And this time, he wondered if it might be trying to tell him something. But what?

The painful memory from earlier that day suddenly surfaced, bringing tears to his eyes. "I told her there's no such thing as magic," Spencer said aloud, each word echoing back to him through the space.

Tears soon overflowed and ran down his cheeks. "I was wrong," he said, realizing that he robbed himself of joy by believing there was only one way to see the world. And he had hurt Emma too.

He thought about all the fun he had over the last couple of hours, and he wished now that Emma had been there with him all along. Not because he could protect her and teach her, but because she had a whole lot she could teach him too. He missed playing with his sister.

Especially make-believe.

And with that, a pink crayon appeared in his hand, and Spencer knew just what he had to do.

He walked confidently across the room to where Izzy and Ollie had disappeared. And where the door had once been, he drew another. This one with a handle at the right and a tiny pink elephant in the upper left corner.

He took a step back to look at it a moment, then stepped up to it again. He added a smile to the elephant's face. And it brought a smile to his own.

Then he wiped the tears from his cheeks and pushed lightly on the door.

It fell open easily.

And he walked on through to the other side.

# 27

# The Explorers of Lost Lane

A few hours ago, Spencer would have been surprised to see a tiny elephant. But now, somehow the sight of the small elephant didn't surprise him at all. Neither did it surprise him to see it surrounded by Emma, Ollie, and Izzy. What did surprise him, however, was that the tiny elephant appeared to be clumsily dressed in a homemade dog costume.

Hours ago he also might have hollered at her for running off like she did. But now he felt more like running up to hug her. He decided on something in between.

"I like your dog," he said as he approached. He

really meant it, and he knew Emma could tell.

"Thanks," she said. I knew Mom and Dad wouldn't let us keep an elephant, but they might let us keep a dog."

Spencer patted the elephant on the head, and it fluttered its tail like it was trying to wag it. This he might have normally questioned, but his mind was still on Emma. "I'm sorry about earlier. Let's not fight anymore, okay?" And he reached down, deciding on the hug after all.

"Okay," she said, hugging him back.

"Besides," he added, "you were right."

"Yeah, I told you," she said, now smiling.

Spencer smiled back. "Yeah, you did. I promise I'll listen more from now on."

The elephant barked playfully, and Spencer turned to see Belaphant now chasing her tail.

Emma giggled. "I taught her that."

"That's a teachable trick?" Izzy said. "Fascinating!"

Emma scratched the elephant behind the ears, and its tongue lolled out the side of its mouth. "Good dog, Belaphant."

"So where are we?" Spencer asked, turning to

look around. For the first time in hours, he was not surrounded by four white walls. Instead, he was outside, in a wildflower field that appeared to stretch on for miles.

"Belaphant brought me here. Maybe this is where tiny elephants come from?" Emma said.

"You think there could be more?" Izzy said, curious as ever.

Emma shrugged. "Maybe."

"Maybe this is Lost Lane?" Ollie said, meeting Spencer's eyes.

"Maybe," he answered. "But shouldn't we be able to see our houses from here?"

"I think this is going to require further exploration," Izzy said.

Spencer was still gazing around at the vastness of the space around them, thinking about the closet he had come through and the magic room they had just left. "It could take years," he said.

"It could take all of us," Izzy said.

"She's right," Emma answered.

Ollie looked at Spencer. "You in?"

Spencer didn't hesitate. "Definitely."

# 28

# Goodnight, Belaphant

"I hate to break it to everyone," Izzy said, "but we still don't know the way home."

"And if our parents aren't home yet, they will be home any minute. How are we supposed to explain where we've been?" Spencer added.

"It's okay, everyone," Emma announced. "Belaphant knows the way. We just need to follow her."

The little elephant had lain down in the grass, but she got up now and walked out in front of the group.

"See?" Emma said. "Everyone, follow Belaphant."

"You don't think there's any chance that she's gonna lead us right back into that puzzle room again, do you?" Ollie said to Spencer as they followed the elephant through the wildflower field.

Spencer shook his head. "I don't think we have to worry about the room anymore. I think I've finally got it figured out."

Izzy and Emma followed along beside Belaphant the elephant, directly ahead of the boys. "So," Izzy said to the little elephant as they walked, "you wouldn't happen to be the one who's been knocking around inside my walls, are you?"

The little elephant smiled, and Izzy laughed. "Okay, but try to keep it down at night. And maybe when my parents are around. I don't think they would understand." The little elephant winked, and Izzy laughed again. "I really like your elephant," she said to Emma.

Emma beamed. "Thanks. I like your pigtails."

"Right back at you," Izzy said, smiling.

The elephant led the way back to a doorway that appeared to hang in midair, and she and the children stepped through, back into the magic room. But Spencer was right: this time it did not contain a puzzle. Rather, the room was filled with balloons and a large sign on the far wall that read, "Welcome Explorers!"

"Incredible!" Izzy said, gazing around. "Truly incredible!"

"Awesome!" Emma exclaimed, walking through curly ribbons that hung down from helium balloons covering the ceiling overhead and kicking at balloons that covered the floor. "This is fantastic!"

Spencer and Ollie smiled happily as they gazed around. Then Spencer said, "Unfortunately, we still need to get home before our parents beat us there. But we'll be back."

And with that, a staircase appeared on the wall to the right, with a door at the top and another sign that said, "Come back soon!"

Once again, the elephant led the way, but when they reached the top, Spencer said, "Hang on, Belaphant." Then he turned to Emma. "Look, I really like her costume, and I would love to have Belaphant around all the time.

But I think this place and everything from it is probably best left just for us. I don't want to say it, but Belaphant needs to stay here. I don't think Mom and Dad would understand."

Emma drooped her head. She tried to come up with an idea to keep the elephant with her, but in the end, she decided Spencer was right. Belaphant would have to stay in the magic room.

Emma stooped down and tried not to cry. "You're a good dog, Belaphant. I will see you tomorrow. And I promise I'll bring you two peanut butter and jelly sandwiches. Oh wait! No," she said, quickly turning back to her brother. "We still don't have any peanut butter." Her lower lip pouted out as tears welled in her eyes.

"No worries," Ollie said. "We got you covered."

Emma smiled and the tears ran down her cheeks. She quickly wiped them away, then reached down and hugged Belaphant around the neck.

Belaphant waggled happily.

"Goodnight, Belaphant," each of the children called and waved as they stepped back through Emma's closet and into her room.

The elephant smiled and headed back down the stairs into the magic room below, where a puppy bed appeared. Spencer watched Belaphant climb into it just before he shut the closet door.

"So," Izzy said to Emma, "mind if I come by to visit you and Belaphant tomorrow?"

Emma looked ecstatic. "Sure! We can walk home together if you want."

Izzy happily agreed.

Meanwhile, Spencer asked Ollie if he thought they would be joining them for the final days of the school year and if he had a partner yet for track and field day.

"Not yet," Ollie said. "But I've always wanted to try that three-legged race. You wanna do it?"

Spencer smiled. Suddenly, track-and-field day didn't seem like such a drag after all.

* * *

That night, as the children lay in bed, they

thought of their new friends, the incredible things that had happened that day, and all the exciting adventures they knew lay ahead.

As he fell asleep that night, Spencer dreamt of a magical room, a tiny elephant, a world of adventure, and three great friends to share it with. And that was the best night's sleep he had in a very long time.

# Discussion Questions & Activities

1. Which character do you resemble most? Spencer, Ollie, Izzy, or Emma?

2. Why do you think Spencer found it so difficult to believe?

3. If you entered the magic room, what do you think you would find?

4. *Illustrate it!* Take any scene from the story and draw what you think it would look like. (Need an idea? How about Belaphant dressed like a puppy dog?)

## From the Authors

Since we first conceived the idea for the Explorers of Lost Lane back in 2015, the characters have taken on a life of their own. They have already explored many places in our imaginations, and we look forward to sharing those stories and places with you in the years to come!

# About the Authors

Amy Joy and CN (Christian) James are a married writing team...

**Amy Joy** is a multi-genre bestselling author and illustrator of young adult and children's lit, specializing in unputdownable fiction. She made her debut into children's literature with "What Happens Next?"™ Fairy Tales.

**CN James** is the author of several novels for young adults, as well as over two dozen popular guitar method books, under the name Christian J. Triola. *The Magic Room* is his first adventure into the world of writing children's fiction.

## We Think you'll Also Enjoy

Choose where the story goes with "What Happens Next?"™ books. Over twenty different endings in each book gives you stories to explore again and again!

What's sillier than a pea in a bed? How about a pizza? Or a dress filled with itching powder? This and more silliness is to come in this new take on Hans Christian Andersen's "The Princess and the Pea."

A frog drummer, a prince with a little extra hop in his step, a frog that loves bubble baths, and much more fun awaits in this new adaptation of the The Grimm Brother's classic tale "The Frog Prince."

Learn more at tenterhookbooks.com.

Made in the USA
Columbia, SC
20 August 2020